The Almond Bark Candy Christmas Caper

Almond Inn Cozy Mysteries

The Prequel

Jamie Gerry

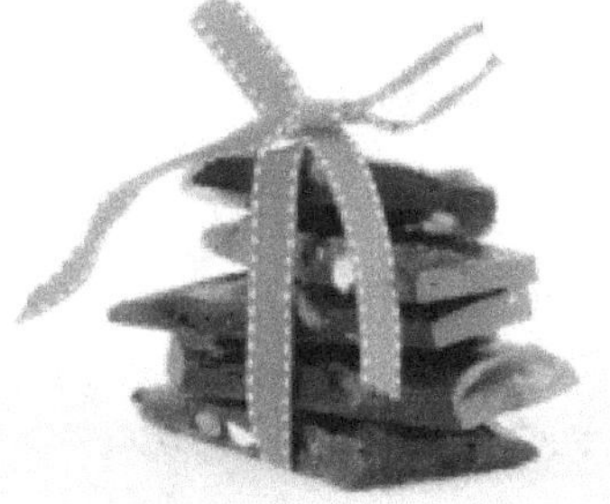

Copyright

Copyright 2023 by Jamie Gerry

Cover Art by pro_design_up

Somes Images by CanvasSlovenia from **Pixabay**

The Ozarks image from The Pottery Shop in Clinton, AR

Table of Contents

Disclaimer 1

Author's Note 3

Chapter One 5

Chapter Two 13

Chapter Three 21

Chapter Four 27

Chapter Five 35

About The Author 45

Also By Jamie Gerry 47

Earlier titles written as Jamie Hill 49

Natalie Almond is a smart cookie with a big problem—she just can't tell her friends no, even when their half-baked ideas involve the words "sneak" and "don't tell." She couldn't back in 1994 and she still can't today. And that, folks, leads up to some fully baked trouble.

Welcome to the Almond Inn Cozy Mysteries. The prequel takes us back thirty years, when Natty and her friends are eleven and turn the Baptist Church upside down and inside out.

Book one in the series, *Getting Toasted in Almond*, is set in the present day, when Natty and her friends have grown-up mysteries to solve!

Disclaimer

This is a work of fiction. Any similarity to actual persons, living or dead, or actual events, is purely coincidental.

Almond, Arkansas is a fictional location set near the real Greer's Ferry Lake and Clinton, Arkansas, "Where the South meets the Ozarks".

Author's Note

Why *Almond, Arkansas*?

Creating a fictional town is easier than using a real location and having everyone in town believe you're writing about them. Plus, I would have a crisis of conscience killing off the local barber. The name Almond had a nice ring to it, and seemed just as good as some of the Arkansas names that were already taken.

(This is coming from someone who used to live in Rose Bud, happily located between Joy and Romance.

I'm currently situated near Shirley, Bee Branch, and Pee Dee!)

So let's cross West Hog Thief Creek and take a spin down Tater Hill Road. But hold on to your hats, the roads are twisty-turnier than a car careening over Rollercoaster Hill!

Please note: The Almond Bark Christmas Candy Caper is the prequel to my new series, The Almond Inn Cozy Mysteries. The prequel is set in 1994, when Natalie Almond and her friends were eleven, to give readers a taste of their childhood. The first book in the series, *Getting Toasted in Almond*, is set in the present day.

Natalie and the other wacky characters in Almond have mysteries to solve, so all y'all come on along! You never know who might end up at the bottom of Greer's Ferry Lake wearing concrete overshoes.

Chapter One

December, 1994
Almond, Arkansas

"Natty Almond, where are you?" Her grandmother's shrill voice could be heard a solid block in all directions. That was basically the point, because Grammy Lena could never be *quite sure* where Natty had gotten off to.

The bed and breakfast inn that the Almond family owned for fifty years was smack dab in the middle of Almond, Arkansas, a small town struggling to reach five hundred people on a sunny day. Her Papaw Cliff said one of his cousins twice removed had named the town, but he'd never produced the proof to say exactly who that was, or what the heck twice removed meant.

Natty didn't care. Living with her grandparents at the Almond Inn was the only thing she'd known in her eleven years, and while some folks said it was unusual, Natty liked that there was always something going on. Even if her mama didn't feel the same way. Her mama *tolerated* the inn and mostly tolerated her folks.

Natty's best friend Vivian lived one street over, and when Natty wasn't at the inn she could often be found at the Vincent house. The "V" family, everyone called them, because Virgil and Valerie Vincent had named their kids Vivian, Violet, and Victor. Natty knew her mama thought it was goofy, and often said so, but Natty thought it was cool. There were times she wished her hair was as red as all the Vincents, and maybe she could have been another child of theirs, with a classy name...something like....*Vanessa.*

"Natalie Suzanne Almond!" Grammy's voice rang out one pitch higher, drawing Natty out of her daydream. She knew when her full name was invoked it was time to answer.

She poked her head in a side door of the inn, which led to the large kitchen. "I'm here."

"Land sakes, child. Where were you?" Grammy's tone softened.

Natty felt a quick pang of guilt. Grammy and Papaw didn't ask much of her, but they did like her to stay close and check in every now and again. Grammy said that ever since the three Cub Scouts were murdered in West Memphis the year before, Arkansas parents hugged their kids just a bit tighter.

"Sorry. I was just sittin' and thinkin'. Maybe gonna go over to Vivi's to sit and think awhile there."

Grammy patted a stack of colorful bags on the counter before her. "Yes, go get Vivian and y'all bring that little red wagon of her brother's back here. I've got another load of almond bark candy I want you girls to take over to the church for me."

"More?" Natty rolled her eyes. "How much more candy are you gonna make?"

Grammy shrugged. "Until we get those Christmas boxes filled I won't know for sure."

Papaw stuck his head around the corner. "Y'all can't tell me the pastor hasn't been eating some of that candy. Last Sunday his pants looked tight."

"Cliff, stop!" Grammy waved a hand to shush him. "He can eat as much as he wants. Lord knows he's earned it, trying to keep sinners like you in line."

He stepped behind her and circled her waist with his hands. Putting his mouth to her ear, he sang softly, "Amazing grace, how sweet the sound, that saved a wretch like me!"

She tried to shrug him off but he wrapped her in a bear hug and Grammy seemed to melt in his arms.

Natty scowled. "Yuck. I'm gonna go get Vivi and the wagon. We'll be back." She scooted toward the door.

"We'll be here!" Papaw called after her.

Natty stole a glance back and saw her grandparents kissing, She screwed up her face.

She was still scowling when she arrived at the Vincent house and saw Vivian, her sister, and her brother helping their daddy unload groceries from the car.

"Who licked the red off your candy?" Mr. Vincent made a pretend pout at her.

Natty shook her head. "Grammy and Papaw. They were smoochin' right there in the kitchen!"

"Ooooh," Vivian, Violet, and Victor all chimed in. "Gross!"

Mr. Vincent laughed. "Your grandparents aren't that old, Natty." He handed her a brown paper bag to carry in the house.

"They're ancient! In their fifties!" She trudged into the house behind the siblings as Mr. V. slammed the trunk of his car and followed them in.

"Fifty is not old, young lady. Fifty is the prime of life! Your kids are finally out of the house, and you have time to be a couple again." He hesitated. "Well, except in your grandparents' case."

Natty set her grocery bag on the kitchen counter and nodded. "Yeah, they say my mama failed to launch, then they laugh like that's hilarious. I don't even know what it means."

"Never mind kiddo. You and your mama are right where you need to be. Your Grammy and Papaw wouldn't have it any other way."

She shrugged, still not really understanding what he meant. "They want to know if Vivi and I can use the red wagon to take some more almond bark candy down to the church."

Victor piped up, "It's my wagon! I wanna go!"

"Aw, Daddy," Vivian began to complain.

He held up one hand like a stop sign. "Not this time, Junior. The girls need to get the candy to the church and back before it gets dark. You and Violet can help me put away the groceries and maybe, if you act real nice, Grammy Lena will send a little bag of bark candy back for us." He raised his eyebrows at Natty.

She grinned. "I expect that can be arranged." She turned to Vivian. "Let's go!"

They jogged outside and Vivian snatched the handle of her brother's Radio Flyer red wagon. She dragged it after her as they headed down the sidewalk for half a block, then cut through ol' man Jenkins' yard as a shortcut to the inn.

His schnauzer, Albee, sounded the alarm as the girls shuffled past his fenced-in play yard, his bark high-pitched and not very threatening.

"Hey, Albee," both girls called to him.

The brown ball of fluff with legs stopped barking and wagged his tail.

They passed on by, almost to the inn.

"I wish CeCe was here," Vivian said.

Natty nodded in agreement. They were the three musketeers, CeCe blonde, Vivi red-headed, and Natty brunette. Of all of them, CeCe was the most outgoing and came up with the best ideas. Everything was more fun when CeCe was around. Tough thing was, CeCe and her mama lived on the other side of town in a trailer park. Neither Vivi's parents or Natty's grandparents would let them play at CeCe's house because her mama wasn't usually home. At night when CeCe's mama tended bar, she hired a babysitter to stay with CeCe. Grammy said that woman slept with her head in a bottle, whatever that meant. Natty just knew it wasn't a good thing.

"Maybe y'all can spend the night with me. I'll ask Grammy!"

"Yay!" Vivi cheered and increased her speed for the last leg of the trek.

Back at the inn, Grammy loaded the wagon with bags of candy, then tucked in two extra bags. "Now, here's a special bag for the pastor, don't be telling your papaw, he might call me fresh. And here's a bag for Victor and the family for the use of the wagon. Run along now. Pastor Pete is expecting you so no dawdling, straight there and back. If you aren't back by four-thirty, I'll send Papaw looking for you and it won't be pretty." She made a 'he's crazy' gesture and screwed up her face.

Natty took the bait. "What's he gonna do, Grammy?"

"He's liable to knock you into the middle of next week lookin' both ways for Sunday!"

Both girls laughed and headed out the door. "Okay, we'll skedaddle."

"Ask her," Vivi nudged Natty.

"Oh, hey! Can Vivi and CeCe spend the night?"

Grammy seemed to think about it for a moment. "I don't see why not. All y'all will hafta go to church with us in the mornin', of course."

"What about CeCe? You think her mama will let her come?"

Grammy waved a hand. "I'll call her. Your daddy may have to pick her up, though," she said to Vivi. "You know Papaw doesn't like drivin' after dark."

Both girls let out a high-pitched whoop as they guided the wagon out the door.

The church was one block over and a few houses down. *One thousand feet*, Papaw, a deacon, always said. *Such a blessing,*

Grammy always said. *Too damned close*, Natty's mama, Melissa, always said.

Pastor Pete was waiting at the door of the Almond Southern Baptist Church. He smiled, which caused his dark brown mustache to wiggle, and he knew it. "Greetings, Miss Natalie and Miss Vivian! And what is that delightful aroma coming from your wagon today?"

Natty dragged the wagon in front of her and stopped it. "Same thing as the last five times, Pastor Pete. The world's best almond bark candy made with love by Grammy Lena. Here's a special bag for you, our little secret." She winked at him.

His laugh was raucous. "Well bless your hearts. Okay, girls, let's get this candy stowed in the basement with all the other gifts for the Operation Christmas Child boxes. Last year was the first year of the program, and we packed twenty shoeboxes. I make the bold prediction that our church can pack thirty this year!"

They went around to the side of the church building and the pastor unlocked the walkout door to the basement. He led them inside and flipped the lights on, then pointed to a row of shelves. "The candy is going over here. We have to keep it separate because the OCC boxes don't allow food."

"Why not?" Vivi asked.

"Oh, most of them go to very warm climates, and it would sure be a disappointment for the children to open a box full of melted candy! Plus, we never know if a child might be allergic to something edible. We would hate to give a gift that could make someone sick. Therefore, we save the candy and treats from the other ladies in the church for local events and activities all throughout the month."

Natty looked at him skeptically. "Does Grammy know that?"

He laughed again. "Yes, she does. She just won't take no for an answer. *'A generous person will prosper; whoever refreshes others will be refreshed.'* ~ Proverbs 11:25."

They unloaded the wagon then made their way back outside. The pastor closed the door but it popped open again. He wrestled with it for a minute, finally leaning into it with his hip and forcing it closed while he locked it. "I'll be leaving after services tomorrow for a few days. If you want to bring more candy, the key to this door is in Miss Mabel's top desk drawer, just outside my office. Please make sure you get it locked tight and put the key back where you found it."

"Yes, sir!" The girls waved and headed home, one wagon and one bag of candy in tow.

Chapter Two

"Let's do it!" Cecilia Crum tossed one blonde pigtail over her shoulder and blew on her wet pink nail polish.

"Tonight?" Natty studied her thumbnail that CeCe had polished but she'd already smudged.

"Lick it," CeCe advised.

"Huh?"

"Lick your nail. It smooths the polish. Mama told me so."

Natty was skeptical, but she licked her thumbnail. "Gross!" It tasted awful, but when she looked at it, the polish had smoothed over a bit.

CeCe grabbed Natty's hand and examined the nail. "I didn't say eat it. See? It worked. Now just sit there and don't fidget until they dry."

Natty got up and paced. "I ain't sure I know how *not* to fidget. I ain't a nail-paintin' kind of a girl."

Vivi admired her freshly painted pink fingertips. "I love it. I just can't do it myself."

CeCe jumped up and grabbed a pink feather boa from her overnight bag. She tossed it around her neck and over one shoulder. "When I grow up I'm never gonna hafta paint my own nails. I'm gonna have someone come in and paint them a different color every day. My toes too. And they'll fix my hair to like look just like Jennifer Anniston."

"Well ain't you Miss Fancy Pants," Natty teased her. She'd heard it before. CeCe wasn't sticking around. As soon as she was out of school, she was out of Almond.

"Darn tootin'!" CeCe grinned. "So are we goin', or what?"

"Tonight?" Natty repeated. She glanced out her bedroom window. It was eight p.m. and dark as pitch. "Where do you wanna go?"

A nervous expression crossed Vivi's face. "I don't think we should sneak out."

"Oh, come on." CeCe rolled her eyes. "Y'all are scaredy cats. I go out after dark all the time. Once Miss Gloria thinks I'm in bed, she puts on her TV shows and fixes a toddy, and she don't even know I'm gone."

"Where do you go?" Natty wondered if CeCe was telling the truth.

"Mostly to the playground in the trailer park. I swing, and sometimes if the Roofus brothers from next door are there we shoot some hoops. But if them older kids from the other side of the park show up we leave real quick. Denny Roofus says they smoke loco weed and are up to no good."

Natty chuckled. "So basically you're the scaredy cat."

CeCe thought about it for a moment, then laughed. "Yeah, I guess so! If Denny doesn't want to be around them, I figure I shouldn't either. I might be a kid, but I ain't stooo-pid." She drew out the word for effect.

Natty's bedroom door opened and her mama slumped against the door frame, her face drawn. "Well, that's good to hear. I wouldn't want my girl hanging around with stooo-pid kids!" Melissa repeated the exaggeration and the girls all laughed. "How's it going in here? Did Grammy feed you dinner?"

They nodded. Natty said, "You worked late."

Her mama nodded. "'Tis the season. And nowhere is it more joyful than in the aisles of your local Kmart Supercenter." She pretended to grab a microphone and said in her best customer service voice, "Look up and look around, Kmart shoppers, that blue light is now flashing in the toy department, where for the next fifteen minutes we have all Mighty Morphin' Power Ranger Action Figures on sale for fifty percent off. That's right! Fifty percent off the regular sale price. So ya'll come on over—wait a second, ma'am, don't push now! Hey, lady, don't shove that child! Excuse me! Ma'am! Give that toy back to that little boy! Oh, for land's sake!"

The girls doubled over with laughter. "Really, Mama?" Natty cackled.

Melissa nodded. "Now mind you, it was nothin' compared to the Great Cabbage Patch Doll Fiasco of '84, where arms were actually broken fightin' to get a doll, but it was close."

Natty shook her head. "Who would fight over a stupid ol' doll?"

Her Mama placed her hands over her heart. "I loved my Cabbage Patch Doll."

Vivi and CeCe's eyes lit up with adoration.

"I am exhausted," Melissa sighed, "But I did stop by Blockbuster and rented Home Alone 1 and 2. I tried to get Christmas Vacation but it was checked out. Maybe next weekend." She nodded towards the other room. "Grab your gear and I'll make some popcorn."

Squealing, the girls gathered all the pillows and blankets their arms could carry. Grammy and Papaw had created a private living space for the family with a fireplace, two recliners, and a sofa sectional. But Natty's favorite part was a *huge* thirty-six-inch TV with a VCR so they could watch videos and record shows, then watch them later.

As they settled in to watch the first movie, Natty glanced around. Her Grammy was crocheting with one eye on the yarn, another on the movie, and somehow still managing to watch the girls. (Natty wasn't sure how she did that, but she always did.) Papaw was already softly snoring in his chair. And her mama, who could have had an easy job helping run the inn except she couldn't get along with her parents well enough to do that, would be slipping outside for a cigarette or two before sleep got the best of her and she'd spend the night on the sofa.

Just then Natty remembered that CeCe had wanted to sneak out. "Is this okay?" she whispered to her friend, on their pile of blankets atop the floor.

"This is great," CeCe said contentedly and snuggled into a stack of pillows.

When Sunday services were over and the girls had finished helping Grammy clean up the dinner dishes, she agreed they could go back to the church and play on the playground in the back for an hour. It was mild weather for early December, and the girls would jump at any chance to get outside. Natty knew that Papaw and some of the other deacons would be putting up some outside Christmas lights at some point, so Grammy felt safe letting them go.

After thirty minutes of swinging and sliding, CeCe got bored and began nosing around the church building. "I don't see anyone here."

Natty glanced around. "Me either. They'll be comin' along shortly I suppose."

CeCe's eyes lit up. "Let's go look at the toys for the Christmas boxes. You said Pastor Pete showed you where the stuff is."

Natty frowned. "He did...but I don't think we're supposed to go in there for no reason."

"We ain't gonna hurt anything. No harm in just lookin.'"

Natty glanced at Vivi, who shrugged.

With a funny feeling in her gut, Natty led them around to the front of the church where they found the office door unlocked. The keys to the basement were in Miss Mabel's desk drawer, right where Pastor Pete said they'd be. She took one last look at CeCe. "We ain't gonna take anythin', right? Just look?"

"Just look." CeCe nodded in agreement.

They tiptoed out of the church stealthily and went around to the side of the building. The door unlocked easily and they slipped inside, pulling it closed behind them. Natty fumbled for the light switch and found it, and the neatly stacked packages of treats came into view.

A little further down on the shelves were rows of open boxes of all kinds of different items. They went to them and began investigating. "Crayons, pencils, pens, notebooks, coloring books, erasers," Vivi said.

"Shoes, T-shirts, socks, sunglasses, combs, brushes, soap and washcloths," Natty noted.

Vivi added, "Dolls, stuffed animals, race cars, balls, blocks, frisbees, and mini footballs. Everything is small."

"They have to fit in shoeboxes," Natty reminded. "Christmas shoeboxes."

"Hmmm," CeCe frowned. "I thought there might be something cooler, like a Talkboy or a Gameboy."

Natty and Vivi stared at her.

"What?" CeCe shrugged. "They fit in shoeboxes."

"Cecilia," Natty used her full name on purpose. "The kids these boxes are going to might not even have houses to live in."

Vivi added, "How can you think about giving them a game when they can't afford the batteries for it?"

CeCe dropped the little football she was holding and placed her hands on her hips. "What makes you two so smart?"

Natty looked at Vivi and they grinned. "Because we asked Grammy and Papaw the same questions and that's what they told us."

"Awww!" CeCe laughed and chased them to the door.

Natty slapped at the light switch on her way out, and was surprised to find the door open. "I thought we closed this behind us?"

"We did." Vivi helped her close the door again and they all three leaned into it from the outside. It clicked, but the key wouldn't turn in the lock. "It won't lock!"

"We have to tell someone," Natty said.

"We'll get creamed!" Vivi's eyes widened. "They'll want to know why we were in there."

"We'll just tell them we wanted to see the stuff. It'll be okay, we didn't hurt anything."

CeCe and Vivi both shook their heads. "Your Mama and grandparents are cool, Natty, but my Mama doesn't have patience for me gettin' into mischief." CeCe raised a hand to her brow exaggeratedly. " I won't be able to come over again for a year!"

"Let's just go," Vivi agreed. "Put the key back, and let's go."

Natty's gut was naggin' at her again, but her friends were halfway down the sidewalk without her. "Wait for me!" She ran back into the church, deposited the key where it belonged, and raced back outside. The basement door was closed. It was probably going to be okay. *She hoped.*

Chapter Three

Natty had just finished breakfast Thursday morning when Papaw came into the kitchen, an unhappy expression on his face. "Natalie, did you girls go into the church basement on Sunday afternoon?"

Grammy stepped up beside him and looked at her questioningly.

Natty's guilt poured out with her confession. "I didn't want to, but CeCe asked to see the stuff for the shoeboxes so I snuck into Miss Mabel's drawers for the key and we went into the basement and we thought the door was shut and we just looked—we didn't take anythin'! I made CeCe promise not to take anythin', and she asked why there was balls and crayons and stuff instead of Talkboys and Gameboys so Vivi and I told her what y'all told us about the kids maybe not even havin' houses and she understood and then we left but the door lock didn't want to—lock, that is, and they begged me not to tell 'cause we'd get in trouble for goin' in there and they took off and I snuck the key back and we came home." She took a breath.

Grammy folded her arms across her chest. "Do you realize in that long and rambling sentence you used the word 'snuck' two times? Does that tell you anything young lady?"

"Oh, yes," Natty nodded sincerely. "My gut was hurting real bad there at first. But then a couple days passed and nothin' happened and I kinda figured it might just be okay."

Papaw frowned. "Well, it's *not* okay. A couple of days passed because Pastor Pete was out of town. When he got back to the church this morning the basement door was open, and the basement was a mess. Someone either ate or stole all the almond bark candy and treats the ladies made. And the gifts for the shoeboxes have been dumped onto the floor and rifled through. It's a real mess, Natty. Those gift boxes were supposed to be packed this weekend and now we don't know if the items are even usable."

Natty's heart sank. "We didn't do that, Papaw! I swear we didn't!"

"No swearing in this house," Grammy snapped.

"I know you didn't," her Papaw said in a bit softer tone. "But someone did, and you three were there."

Natty bit her lip. "What's gonna happen?"

He shook his head. "I don't rightly know. I'll take you to school and I guess we'll deal with this later."

She rubbed her belly. "I'm not sure my gut is up to school just now."

Grammy guided her by the shoulders. "Well, pull up your big girl pants and get up to it. You're not getting rewarded for bad behavior and missing school. That mess in the church isn't going anywhere. My guess is, the three of you will be cleaning it up this afternoon for as long as it takes to make things right." She aimed Natty in the direction of the bathroom. "Now go. Brush your teeth, grab your backpack and your lunch. Papaw will be waiting in the truck."

"Yes, Ma'am." Natty did as directed, her feet dragging a slight bit more than usual. No one seemed to notice that *she* hadn't wanted to go into the church basement. CeCe and Vivi wanted to, *not her*. As Natty brushed her teeth, she imagined her friends on their hands and knees in the church basement, picking up trash, while Natty stood above them with a whip and a bullhorn, like a ringmaster at a circus. She smiled, and spit.

She *wasn't* smiling after lunch when her teacher asked her to get her things and head to the principal's office. When she got there, Papaw was waiting with Mr. and Mrs. Vincent and Miss Francie, CeCe's mama. "Wh-what's goin' on?" Natty almost whispered.

Before anyone could speak, CeCe and Vivi joined them with their coats and backpacks in hand.

Papaw spoke first. "Girls, this incident at the church has gotten more serious. It turns out there was some real damage done to the structure of the building, and Pastor Pete has no choice but to file a police report in order to make an insurance claim. Police Chief Hudson wants all of us down at the station so he can get statements from each of you. Because you're minors, your parents will be able to stay with you. But it's very important that you tell the truth. Chief Hudson said if he catches wind that any of you are lyin', he's gonna recommend that we each get lawyers, and that's liable to run into a heap of money per family. We really don't want to do that, now do we?" He gazed at each girl individually.

They shook their heads slowly.

"We're gonna ride down to the station separately and this might be a good time for each family to have a come to Jesus meetin'. I do not wanna go home and tell Grammy we need to find a lawyer for our eleven-year-old reprobate."

Mr. V. added, "Don't want you to end up in the hoosegow!"

His wife patted his shoulder. "Oh, Virgil!"

Papaw snorted. "See all y'all down there." He pointed at Natty and jerked his thumb toward the door.

She scampered out in front of him.

The ride in the truck was better than Natty expected. Papaw said he believed that she hadn't wrecked the church basement, but he wanted to make sure she realized how serious the matter was, and above all else *to tell the truth*.

The Almond Police Department was small, but there were several rooms and Police Chief Hudson separated the three families. Natty had seen the man around town a few times but he was new to town and didn't go to their church, so she didn't know him well. As she sat on a sofa in his office next to Papaw, her guilt gut was churning in full force.

The tall man came in and closed the door behind him, then leaned against the edge of his desk and looked at her. "Hello, Natalie."

"Hello, Sir."

"I understand that your grandmother gave you and your friends permission to play on the church playground last Sunday afternoon. Did she give you permission to go into the building?"

"No, Sir."

"Did you go into the building?"

Papaw spoke with a touch of irritation. "You know she did, Roman."

"I need to hear it from her, Cliff." He turned back to Natty.

"Yes, Sir. Pastor Pete told me and Vivi where he keeps the keys to the basement door, in Miss Mabel's drawer. CeCe wanted to see the toys for the shoeboxes. We just wanted to look at the stuff, we didn't take anything, or bother anything, we just looked at it."

"You didn't take any of that good almond bark candy that was stored in there?"

"Sir, my Grammy makes that candy all season long for guests at the inn. If I want candy all I have to do is walk into the kitchen. If there's none there, a sad set of puppy-dog eyes from either me or Papaw gets a fresh batch on the stove right quick." She looked at her grandfather.

He nodded in agreement.

The police chief sighed and glanced out the window, then back at Natty. "The thing is, you and your friends were the last people seen going into the church basement before the pastor returned and found one heck of a mess. The candy and other food has been eaten and smashed into the floor. The toys and gifts were dumped out and have been damaged beyond repair, almost viciously. Some were ripped to shreds, some were chewed up or torn up, I don't know what, or why. But the worst part is there's damage to the floor and walls where someone has been digging and scratching. The marks are deep. What were you looking for? Or trying to do?"

"We weren't trying to do anything, Sir! I told you, we looked at the toys for maybe five minutes. We knew Papaw and the other deacons were coming to put up some Christmas lights so we didn't want to stay down there too long. We looked and then we left. The door—" Natty hesitated.

"What about the door?"

She spoke slowly. "The door wouldn't lock. All three of us leaned into it and we got it closed, but I couldn't turn the key to lock it. Vivi and CeCe said to leave it, and they took off and headed home. I got scared so I just put the key back and ran home with them."

Papaw's face fell. "Why didn't you tell me, Natty? We know that door sticks. I could have made sure it was locked."

"CeCe was afraid if we got in trouble, her mama wouldn't let her come over for a year."

He exchanged glances with the police chief.

Chief Hudson said, "I think that's all we need for now. I'll get back with you after I've spoken with the other girls. But I have a better picture of what may have gone on, anyway."

Papaw nodded and stood, reached for Natty's hand, and led her out.

Chapter Four

Papaw said it was a good news/bad news kinda situation when the police chief called him later that night. The girls' stories had all been the same, so he didn't suspect any of them were lying. Now the thinkin' was that someone had come in after them and trashed the place, and unfortunately, CeCe's friendship with Denny Roofus and his brothers was the first place they were tempted to look. The Roofus boys were bad news, even if Denny did try to protect CeCe from the older, more nefarious hoodlums.

Chief Hudson said that while the girls probably weren't looking at any time in the hoosegow, they very well could be looking at fines and restitution to make the church whole.

Grammy frowned. "Pastor Pete won't let that happen!"

Papaw shook his head. "It's out of his hands, Lena. With the police and insurance company involved, he has very little to say about it now."

Melissa grabbed her pack of cigarettes and stood to go outside. "A preacher with very little to say, now that's a first!"

"Don't be disrespectful young lady! The church folk don't think this situation is as funny as you seem to."

"Oh, I'm sure their holy tongues are wagging, that's no doubt!"

"They donated hard-earned money for those shoebox gifts and now they're all ruined. What are they supposed to think? And our family name is getting dragged through the mud."

"Cheese and crackers, Mama, just have Daddy write a check and the crappy little gifts can be replaced just like that." She snapped her fingers.

Papaw gave Melissa a cold stare. "Maybe you better head on out for that nicotine fix."

"Maybe I better." She turned to go.

Natty glanced at her. "Can I come with you, Mama?"

She hesitated for just a moment then said, "Grab your jacket."

Natty did as instructed and followed her mama to the back patio. Grammy and Papaw didn't like her Mama smoking on the patio when guests were sitting out there, but it was cold and dark, with no guests in sight. She sat in one Adirondack chair and her mama another, with a small table between them. "I'm sorry about the trouble, Mama."

Melissa lit up a cigarette and took a drag, then blew a long puff of smoke in the opposite direction of her daughter. "I know, baby. Y'all didn't do anything so bad. But apparently, someone came along after you who did, and unless they catch them, you and the girls are going to be stuck paying for the damages."

Natty's eyes widened. "I don't have that kind of money. Well, I have thirty-two dollars and sixty-eight cents I've saved up from chores. Will that help?"

Her mama smiled. "It'll help, baby. But your papaw has the money, don't you worry about it. You'll just be stuck washin' dishes at the inn to pay him back, prolly 'til you're eighteen. But after that girl, I want you to leave Almond and go to college, maybe even leave Arkansas. Get out there and see the world. Don't let anyone make you think you have to stay here out of guilt or any ol' reason."

Natty blinked a few times, trying to understand. She loved the inn and had never considered leaving it. "I don't wanna leave, Mama. I wanna stay here forever."

Her mama's hoarse laugh surprised her. "You say that now. Things will look a lot different when you reach a certain age and start thinkin' about boys and all the different possibilities out there."

Natty mused on that for a minute. "Mama, why didn't you leave, then? You're the one who doesn't like the inn."

Melissa inhaled another long drag, then blew it out slowly. "I don't dislike the inn. It's the feeling of confinement. Like you don't own *it,* it owns *you* and your life, and you can never get away from it." She shrugged. "Grammy and Papaw don't seem to mind that. It gives me the heebie-jeebies."

Natty put her face closer to her mama's. "You didn't answer my question. Why didn't you leave, then? Go see the world?"

Melissa sighed. "Oh, Natty girl, I did leave. I went to Memphis and was working there, saving up to take classes at a beauty school. Then I met your daddy, this wonderful, handsome Marine who was home on leave. We saw each other when we could and baby, we fell in *love*! But he got called into action and had to go to Grenada. *Operation Urgent Fury,* they called it. After that, they put him on a boat and he couldn't say where he was. Broke my heart when he left. We said we'd keep in touch, but I never heard from him again."

Natty hung on every word. She'd asked about her father in the past, but her mama hadn't wanted to talk about him then. *Someday*, she'd always said. "Did you try to find him?"

"Of course I tried! 'specially when I found out that he left me with you." She patted her tummy and smiled.

Natty touched her face like Kevin in the movie Home Alone. "Oh, Mama! What was his name?"

"Jake."

"Jake," Natty repeated dreamily. "But you didn't give me his last name. Don't you usually give the baby the daddy's last name?"

Melissa thought about that. "Usually, I s'pose. It would have been more difficult for you and me going through life with different last names. But the real reason was, I didn't know how to spell it back then. His last name was Kowalczyk."

Natty exchanged glances with her mama and they both laughed. She choked out. "I s'pose I would have learnt how to spell it eventually!"

"Me too!" Melissa chortled.

Grammy joined them on the patio. "Glad to see you girls getting along out here, but it's getting' bitter cold. Shouldn't you come inside? Don't want either of you fallin' sickly."

"I'm ready." Melissa crushed out her cigarette and tucked the butt back into the pack. "How about you, Mizz Almond?"

"Ready, Mizz Almond." Natty put her arm around her mama's waist and they walked together back into the inn.

Friday morning, Chief Hudson was at the Inn before Papaw could drive Natty to school.

"Morning, Roman," Papaw invited him in. "Cup of coffee? Scone?"

"No thank ya Cliff, already had three cups and about ready to float away. I heard something interesting and wanted to run it past Natalie. If you don't mind."

Papaw stepped aside and motioned the chief inside.

Natalie shirked against her grandfather's leg.

He rubbed her shoulder and she felt a little better.

The chief smiled at her. "I ran into Ted Jenkins this mornin' at the Stop and Go. You know him, he lives just down the block a ways?"

She nodded. She *didn't* know his name was Ted. Most people called him "ol' man Jenkins" because he could be kinda cantankerous, especially when Albee escaped his fence and Jenkins had to chase him down. Vivi and she had helped him catch Albee one time, and they'd heard a whole bunch of new words she was quite sure were *not* in the bible.

"Well, he mentioned that he was walking his dog Sunday afternoon and he saw you girls going into the church basement...along with your dog."

"We don't have a dog," Natty spoke up quickly. "Grammy says it wouldn't be right as some of the guests could be allergic.

The Vincents say they have enough kids and don't need another mouth to feed, and CeCe's mama don't like dogs. So none of us has a dog."

The chief looked at Papaw. "Ted is sure he saw a dog follow the girls. He said it was black and brown, possibly a miniature schnauzer because that's what he has. And get this, her belly was hangin' low."

"Huh?" Natty looked from him to her papaw.

"She's pregnant?" Papaw asked the chief.

Chief Hudson shrugged. "If Ted is to be believed. He seems to know his dogs. He also joked about the possibility that his male is the sire, considering the number of times he's run off."

Natty squealed. "She's gonna have puppies? Then we need to find her!"

The chief and her papaw both sighed, and her papaw said, "Honey, Almond is a small town, but the woods around us go for miles and miles. There's a gazillion places a dog could take shelter. If she's ready to give birth she's probably already made her a whelping spot somewhere out of the way and who knows where that could be?"

"Well first," Natty counted on her fingers, "We don't know that she's ready to give birth right this minute. And second, if she was at the church on Sunday, she might—*mind you I said might*—still be in town. What if we set up a stakeout, like they do on The Untouchables?"

"A stakeout?" The chief laughed.

Papaw shook his head. "You've been watching too much TV."

"Grammy watches it with me, and the FBI Files, too. Sometimes the perps come back to the scene of the crime. Think about it. Tonight's Friday night. What if we leave the church basement door open, and sit in a car down the block where no one can see us? We'll use Papaw's birdwatching binoculars and see if anyone takes the bait. If it's them no-good Roofus boys then Chief, you can call for backup, and Papaw and I will stay in the car and let you take 'em down. But if the dog shows up we can try to catch her, and maybe she won't need to have her puppies in a manger somewhere in the cold." She batted her eyelashes.

Chief Hudson held up his hand. "Well first, we don't know that she hasn't already had her pups. And second, if she has, and we catch her, what's going to happen to those poor little puppies out there in the manger all alone with nary one wise man to bring them a gift and their mama all locked up? And third, if them no-good Roofus boys show up, I'm the only backup in Almond, so what do your FBI instincts tell you I should do then?"

She scratched her chin. "I would say, *'Therefore do not worry about tomorrow, for tomorrow will worry about itself. Each day has enough trouble of its own.'* ~ Matthew 6:34."

"Ooh, dirty trick, pulling out the bible on me."

"She knows her bible," Papaw advised. "She can recite 1John, 2John and 3John from memory."

The chief blinked. "But does she understand them?"

"Excuse me!" Natty tapped her toe. "I'm standing right here!"

He looked at her. "So, do you understand them?"

"I reckon as well as you do, considering I ain't never seen you at church, Sir."

He belly laughed at that while Papaw smacked her arm, his face blushing red.

"Fair enough. Fair enough." The chief looked at her. "Okay, Miss Natalie Almond, I'll give you two hours tonight, from seven to nine p.m. for your stakeout."

"I bet them Roofus boys don't even sneak out 'til after nine. Let's say ten p.m., shall we? It is Friday night, after all. I bet I can get Grammy to pack us some cookies and scones, maybe some hot chocolate?"

He glanced at Papaw and with a quick eye roll turned back to Natty. "A thermos of coffee is all I need. And maybe some of that almond bark candy to take home to the family if your grammy is so inclined."

"Yes, Sir! Can we swing by and pick up Vivi? It's prolly too far to get CeCe but—"

"NO, NO, NO," the chief replied sternly. "This is a three-person sting, and those three people are standing right here. I'm not taking the entire cabbage patch with me." He turned toward the door. "I'll pick you up at seven."

"What should we wear?" Natty followed him. "Should we wear black? Or camo gear?"

He turned back to her, forcing a look of patience. "I don't give a hoot what you wear. Wear your pajamas for all I care. I'll see you at seven." He stepped out.

"I don't have any camo p,j.'s," she called after him, and looked up at Papaw. "Think I could call Mama and see if she could check if Kmart has any?"

Chapter Five

It turned out jeans were the uniform of the evening. They rode in the chief's wife's SUV since they were on a stakeout and an unmarked vehicle was called for. Natty kept watch with her cheap set of binoculars for the first thirty minutes, then spent the next thirty minutes *mostly* watching while munching cookies and sipping hot cocoa. After ninety minutes of listening to the two men in the front seat discuss the important city of Almond issues, Natty struggled to stay awake.

Something out the corner of her eye caught her attention, and she bolted upright. "Did you see that?"

"What?" Both men asked.

"The basement door! I saw something."

"I don't think so, sweetie," her grandfather yawned.

"I dunno, Cliff." The chief squinted. "That door does look like it's open more than it was."

"Let's go check it out!" Natty opened her car door.

"Hold your horses there kiddo." The chief grabbed her arm. "You're not goin' anywhere. *I* will check it out, and if there's anything to see I'll give you a sign."

"Okay." She nodded excitedly. "What's the sign?"

He turned back as he walked toward the church. "How about 'come here'?" He made a 'come here' motion with his hand.

Natty gave him an excited thumbs up. She and Papaw watched him intently as he approached the building with his flashlight.

He stepped inside and closed the door behind him. In less than a minute, he stepped out, motioned for them to come over, and went back into the church.

"Well, I'll be. Come on!" Papaw and Natty hopped out, he grabbed her hand and they hurried to the church basement. They slipped inside and both gasped to see the chief sitting on the floor petting a very excited and very pregnant dog.

"She's as sweet as can be," he said, "but she's in bad shape. Looks half-starved to death and matted beyond belief."

Papaw gave her a rub. "No collar I guess."

"Nope. She almost leapt for joy when she saw me."

"Oooh," Natty petted the dog. "What a pretty girl!"

The chief looked worried. "We've gotta get her to the vet. Can you stay with her while I go get the car and bring it closer? I'll call the vet and let her know we're on our way. I'll get the dog settled in the back seat with Natalie while you lock up the church."

"Can do," Papaw nodded.

The chief went for his car and Papaw put one hand on the dog and the other on Natty's cheek. "You saved her, girl."

Natty looked down at the dog. "I dunno, Papaw. She don't look saved yet."

The local vet was a woman who'd grown up in Almond and returned to practice in the county after graduating from veterinary college. She was young but smart and had earned the respect of everyone she dealt with. Natty's family knew her from church and that was all the references they needed.

They'd been in her waiting room for about an hour when Dr. Deb came out for the first time.

"How's she doing?" Chief Hudson stood, as nervous as an expectant father himself.

"She's a trooper. Poor girl, I don't know how she's survived in this weather. It's a blessing it's been a mild winter so far, but the nights still get frigid. And what's she been eating? I'm not surprised when she discovered the treasure trove of treats in the church that she went to town on them. She probably hasn't had a decent meal in ages."

Papaw scratched his head. "Why d'you's'pose she got into the toys and such? The food I understand, but the other stuff? Not so much."

They all shook their heads.

Dr. Deb looked at them. "All y'all might as well go on home. I think she's gonna deliver tonight but I wouldn't bet the farm on it. Only time will tell."

Chief Hudson said, "I'd like to stay if you don't mind. Cliff, take my car on home and leave the keys on the floorboard. The wife can pick me up later, and we'll swing by the inn for the car at some point."

"Sounds good. Let us know in the morning how she's doin', will you?"

"Will do." The chief turned to Natty. "I might have to look into getting you a junior detective badge or something. Good job, young lady."

She smiled sadly. "It's a fine thing that we figured it out, but we don't know if the dog is really okay. The church is still wrecked, and the shoeboxes are all ruined. So frankly, Sir, I don't believe there's much good about it. But I'm plum tuckered out, so I reckon it's a good time for us to go home and go to bed. Night, Sir. Night, Dr. Deb."

"Goodnight Natty," the vet smiled at Papaw as Natty shuffled out to the car.

It was nearly midnight when Natty fell into bed and ten a.m. when she looked at the clock Saturday morning. She heard noise. Not unusual living in an inn, but this was more noise than usual. She rolled out of bed, tucked her feet into her slippers and opened her bedroom door.

"Oh, hey!" Her mama was just coming from her own room.

"Mama? What are you doin' here? On a Saturday 'specially?"

Her mama planted a kiss on the top of her head. "Don't you worry your pretty little head about that. Now, there's lots of guests downstairs so put some clothes on before you come down."

Natty had always been allowed to eat breakfast in the kitchen in her two-piece, flannel pajamas, and started to protest. "But—"

"No buts! Nobody wants to hear 'em! Nobody wants to see 'em! I'm your mama and I'm tellin' you to get dressed and meet me in the kitchen pronto!" She turned and marched off.

Grumbling to herself, Natty returned to her room and pulled some clothes off the floor. Maybe it *was* a good thing her mama was an assistant manager at the Kmart and worked ten-hour days. She'd heard the whispered, heated 'discussions' between her mama and her papaw when mama wanted to move out so she didn't have to make the thirty-minute drive to Clinton every day. Papaw wanted her to stay at the inn so they could watch over her progeny, whatever that was. Natty didn't understand the word, but she could tell they were arguing over it, and they both cared about it very much.

She laced up her last sneaker and skipped down the back stairway to the kitchen. Her jaw nearly hit the floor to find Vivi, CeCe, her Mama, and several other ladies wearing aprons and helping Grammy bake in the large kitchen. "Wh-what's goin' on?"

Grammy smiled at her. "Three batches of almond bark candy done. We've got a lot of catching up to do to replace what was lost."

Vivi added, "We're baking cookies!"

CeCe grinned. "And your mama is gonna show us how to bake a pecan pie!"

"Wow!" Natty struggled to keep her jaw closed.

Her mama said, "There's more, baby. Head on into the lobby there." She nodded toward the front of the inn.

Confused but curious, Natty did as directed. The lobby was a large L-shaped room featuring a massive stone fireplace with two leather chairs in front of it. There were two other seating areas and they were usually plenty for the inn guests. Today, Natty couldn't begin to count the people there. Twenty maybe? It looked like chairs had been brought over from the church. She spotted her Papaw and Pastor Pete, and weaved her way over to them.

"There's my girl! Mornin' Sleepin' Beauty. It was a late night, wasn't it?" Papaw hugged her from the side.

She nodded. "Have you heard anythin' about the dog? Did she have her puppies?"

"We'll find out soon enough. The pastor here has somethin' he wants to tell you."

She gazed up at him.

"Natalie, I have a confession. I have committed the sin of gluttony. Each time you brought a wagon full of almond bark candy, I kept a bag for myself. Now, I couldn't keep it in my office, because Miss Mabel cleans in there religiously, if you'll pardon the pun. So I tucked each bag in a different spot in the basement. Some were in the boxes of toys to go in the shoeboxes. One was in the closet where the utilities are located. I never dreamed a half-starved dog would come in and sniff out every one of those bags. She turned out every box looking for food, and the poor girl must have gone crazy scratching and digging for that last bag in the utility closet."

Suddenly, it all made sense to Natalie. "So it wasn't them no-good Roofus boys?"

Papaw laid a hand on her shoulder. "No, and I believe it's time we stop calling them that, right, *Natalie?*"

She gulped. "Yes, Sir."

He smiled.

Pastor Pete continued. "I spoke to as many members of the church as I could, and confessed my sin. The Lord has blessed our church this year, and we have some extra money in the missions fund. I've agreed to match whatever we need to spend to replace the shoebox items, if folks would come together to help me go get the things. Your grandparents agreed we could use the inn to gather and pack the shoeboxes. The guests are even getting into the spirit by helping out. It's been quite jovial this morning!"

Papaw nodded. "God is good."

"All the time," Pastor Pete and Natty replied in unison.

The front door opened and Chief Hudson came in. He grinned when he saw Natty. "Just the person I was looking for. Grab your coat and come outside with me."

She glanced up at Papaw.

He nodded approval.

She dashed to the back of the inn for her jacket and returned quickly, then followed the chief out to his SUV.

He paused by the back door. "It's too cold to bring her out, but I wanted you to see her before we took her home." He opened the door to the running SUV. The heater was on and it felt nice and toasty inside. There was a large brown box in the seat. Natty leaned in and looked in the box. The dog was lying on her side. She'd been shaved and looked so much better than the mess of mats she'd been the night before. There were several towels around her, and one little lump, so small Natty almost missed it. "A puppy!" A brown and white ball of fuzz. Confused, she examined the towels closer, the looked up at the chief. "Just one?"

He nodded. "She was in bad shape, Natalie. The vet was only able to save one pup. The good news is, both the pup and the mama are doin' fine now. We started her on some healthy food and we'll bottle feed the pup until she starts makin' milk, if she ever does. If she doesn't, we'll feed him. He'll be fine."

"He's so cute! So you're gonna take care of them?"

"We are. We're gonna keep the mama, and as soon as she's healthy enough we're gonna have her spayed, so no more puppies. We're calling her Trooper."

Natty grinned. "That's perfect! But what about the pup?"

He shook his head. "I could only convince the wife we needed one dog. So I guess the pup is going to be yours."

She blinked. "I wish. Grammy said—"

"Whatever your grammy said in the past has changed, young lady. You did a fine thing last night and I believe your family agrees you've earned a puppy." He pointed to the front door of the inn.

Natty looked there and saw her mama and grandparents standing together, smiling and nodding. Her heart grew two sizes at that moment, and she grinned.

She turned back around and said, "You're naming her Trooper? I've always wanted a dog to name Cooper!"

"That would be cool," a voice from the other side of the box said.

Startled, she glanced up. A fella with dark hair, about her age, was holding the box protectively. He had bright blue eyes and an even brighter smile.

The chief said, "Oh, sorry, Natalie, I don't believe y'all have met. This is my son, Jake."

Jake offered a grin and a wave.

Jake.

Natty smiled.

SANTA SAYS:
"IF YOU LIKED THIS BOOK, PLEASE LEAVE A REVIEW WHEREVER YOU PURCHASED IT. IF YOU STOLE IT, YOU CAN LOOK FORWARD TO COAL IN YOUR STOCKING!"

About The Author

Jamie Gerry raised her family in Kansas, then later met a California fella and ended up in Arkansas, *The Natural State*. Sounds only natural, right?

Their whirlwind romance had a few ups and downs but by holding on to the Lord and each other they weathered the storms and both agree they are now in a very good place.

Jamie spends her days helping authors self-publish their books and squeezes some time in the evenings creating tales of her own. When her face is not in front of a computer screen, Jamie likes to spend time with her husband, family, and friends. She proudly sings in the Baptist choir (*"Sing and make music from your heart to the Lord."~ Ephesians 5:19b)*, and she enjoys being crafty, crocheting, word puzzles, and snuggling with her fur babies Dory and Enzo (or 'white dog' as her youngest grandson calls him!)

Life in Arkansas is good.

Also By Jamie Gerry

The Almond Inn Cozy Mysteries Book 1, *Getting Toasted in Almond.*

Celia Masterson hasn't lived in Almond since she was a little girl named CeCe Crum, 'cause one day she and her Mama took the last train to Clarksville and never looked back. Celia managed to meet the right person and strike it big acting in television commercials. Now she's managed to anger the *wrong* person and a little downtime in Almond with her old friends Natalie Almond and Vivian Clark may be just what she needs to get away from it all. Only problem is—there's been a death in Almond. Two of them, to be precise. One was sad and not unexpected. The other was unexpected and not very sad.

There's plenty of space in the Ozarks to hide a body. The only question is, what's the new police chief Jake Hudson plan to do? Question the girls, or bring another shovel?

https://books2read.com/gettingtoastedinalmond

Earlier titles written as Jamie Hill

Available in Print, Ebook and Apple Store-only A.I.-Narrated Audiobooks.
https://books2read.com/ap/xqlaam/Jamie-Hill
Romantic Suspense Titles

A Cop in the Family Series

Family Secrets
Family Ties
Family Honor

Witness Security Series

Pieces of the Past
Time to Kill
Cover of Darkness

On The Edge (novella)

On The Edge (novella)

Romance Titles

Secrets and Lies
Unexpected Love Trilogy

The Blame Game Series

Blame it on the Stars
Blame it on the Moon
Blame it on the Sun
Blame it on the Rain

Don't miss out!

Visit the website below and you can sign up to receive emails whenever Jamie Gerry publishes a new book. There's no charge and no obligation.

https://books2read.com/r/B-A-BYRBB-AIERC

BOOKS 2 READ

Connecting independent readers to independent writers.

About the Publisher

'Pets Rescue Us' Publishing

Before you purchase a pet, please consider a shelter animal. The cost may be cheaper and the rewards may be greater! Rescue = Love.